Running the Point

PRAISE FOR *STORYSHARES*

"One of the brightest innovators and game-changers in the education industry."
– Forbes

"Your success in applying research-validated practices to promote literacy serves as a valuable model for other organizations seeking to create evidence-based literacy programs."

- Library of Congress

"We need powerful social and educational innovation, and Storyshares is breaking new ground. The organization addresses critical problems facing our students and teachers. I am excited about the strategies it brings to the collective work of making sure every student has an equal chance in life."
– Teach For America

"Around the world, this is one of the up-and-coming trailblazers changing the landscape of literacy and education."
- International Literacy Association

"It's the perfect idea. There's really nothing like this. I mean wow, this will be a wonderful experience for young people."   - Andrea Davis Pinkney, Executive Director, Scholastic

"Reading for meaning opens opportunities for a lifetime of learning. Providing emerging readers with engaging texts that are designed to offer both challenges and support for each individual will improve their lives for years to come. Storyshares is a wonderful start."
- David Rose, Co-founder of CAST & UDL

Running the Point

Simon Broder

STORYSHARES

Story Share, Inc.
New York. Boston. Philadelphia

Storyshares
Story Share, Inc.
24 N. Bryn Mawr Avenue #340
Bryn Mawr, PA 19010-3304
www.storyshares.org

Inspiring reading with a new kind of book.

Interest Level: High School
Grade Level Equivalent: 3.9

9781642614749

Book design by Storyshares

Printed in the United States of America

Storyshares Presents

1

The old Toyota behind the warehouse was Ennie's fortress. It was a hollowed out husk of a wreck with doors that refused to open, two missing tires, and a smashed driver's side window. In the back seat, Ennie had stashed a BB gun, a Swiss army knife, and a ratty old copy of *Sports Illustrated* with Russell Westbrook on the cover. Westbrook was his favorite player.

A patchy, crooked wire fence separated the alleyway from the parking lot, and despite the fact that the cars parked only a dozen feet away, the fence made the mountain of junk that surrounded the car seem isolated from civilization. Sometimes Ennie wondered if the rotting lumber and broken bricks were important ruins left over from when the city had first been settled. Other times he liked to imagine that he could use them to build his own house far away from his Aunt Lucía one day.

His *tía* was a strict Mexican lady with a sharp tongue. The last time she'd caught him in the alley she had grounded him for a week and warned him about all sorts of horrible diseases. Still, risking her wrath was worth getting the thrill of exploring the unknown worlds of the laneway.

But today, he wasn't interested in any of that. Today, he had come back here to forget about the way that Troy had embarrassed him. Troy was the tallest kid in basketball camp, and when he'd spotted Ennie this morning he'd poured a whole bottle of Gatorade down his shirt. That was bad enough, but even worse was the way he dominated Ennie in the one-on-one drill. Ennie was quick with his dribble and always bragged that he would be the next Westbrook, but the scrimmage had ended without Ennie scoring even a single point over the fourteen-year-old's massive reach.

Ennie reached the car and climbed through the broken window. But his bag of belongings was not where he left them in the back seat. He only found a ratty blanket and a few empty bags of Chinese noodles.

Ping.

The metallic clatter radiated through the vehicle. Ennie didn't know where it came from, but it sounded ominous. He flattened himself amongst the weeds that poked through the Toyota's rusted-out undercarriage.

Ping.

The sound came again, but this time it sounded oddly familiar. There was no doubt that something was hitting against the car.

"Hey!" Ennie yelled. "Stop that."

"Who are you?" The voice was high-pitched but raw. It was not a voice Ennie recognized.

"Who are *you?*" Ennie retorted.

"Whatcha doing here?"

"I always come here."

"So what, this your gun then?"

Ennie realized nervously that the pinging was coming from the BB gun that should have been waiting for him in the backseat. He'd seen what BB gun pellets could do. And the old car didn't make for a very reliable fort.

"Yeah, it's mine," he said. "Don't shoot anymore!"

"Aw... right," the voice came, trembling slightly. "But ain't ya gonna be mad that I stole it?"

"No," Ennie said. "Just stop."

"Promise?"

"Yeah, I promise!" Ennie shouted. "Who are you?"

2

A gap-toothed, pale face with streaks of dirt and a forehead covered in bright red pimples appeared in the driver's side window. At first Ennie thought it was a teenage boy, but when she brushed her ratty yellow hair out of her eyes he realized he'd been wrong.

"'Sup?" the dirty girl beamed, holding the handle of the BB gun out for him. "I'm Kelly."

Once Ennie got a good look at Kelly, he realized he liked her. She seemed different from anyone he'd ever seen before. She seemed friendly. But something was off about her. Ennie looked from Kelly's grubby face to the dirty blanket in the back seat.

"You live here?" Ennie asked.

"Only sorta," Kelly shrugged. "I'm supposed to live with my pops, but he don't like me much. So I been staying here since the weekend."

"Wow, I never knew anyone who lived in a car before."

Now that he had secured his BB gun, Ennie started to pick through the junk looking for the rest of his things. He found the *Sports Illustrated* blown up against the fence, but when he picked up the magazine, he saw that there was a tear in the cover right through Westbrook's face. He clutched the ripped magazine to his chest.

"You gonna save that old rag?" Kelly said.

"This is gonna be me one day," Ennie said, pointing at Westbrook's picture.

"It's all torn up."

"Well, it wasn't before you got your hands on it."

Kelly shrugged. "Oops."

He asked Kelly if she had his Swiss army knife.

"Naw," she said, but she put her hand in her jeans pocket when she said it and Ennie saw the outline of the multi-tool.

"C'mon," he said. "It's mine."

"So what, we friends or ain't we?" she said.

"Sure, we're friends."

"You're too small to be a basketball player," she said dismissively.

Ennie remembered the way Troy had loomed over him. He didn't like that she'd said that. Before he knew what he was doing, he reached his hand into her pocket and started running towards the street.

"I might be small, but I'm quick," he yelled back.

Ennie had almost made it out of the alley when his foot caught on a spare tire and he crashed into the fence. Kelly dove for the knife but it skittered under some metal rods. When Ennie sat up, he had a gash the size of a plum on the back of his elbow.

"You alright?" Kelly said, forgetting the knife. She pried his fingers away from his elbow to examine the wound. "It's just a scrape."

"It hurts, though."

"Oh, ya big baby. You want me to walk you home?"

3

"Enrique!" Lucía was screeching. "What were you doing?"

His *tía* had him seated on the concrete step in the backyard of the townhouse they shared. She was a round, brown woman with a wild nest of dreadlocks on her head and a plain yellow dress that went down to her knees. She was rinsing out his wound with rubbing alcohol, and despite Ennie's best efforts to wriggle away from the pain, her grip on his arm held firm.

"It's nothing, *tía*," he winced. "It's just from... playing ball."

"Ennie," Lucía said, taking his chin firmly in her hand. "Were you playing behind the warehouse again?"

"Yes, *tía*," Ennie sullenly admitted.

"*Por favor,* Enrique! You know what I told you about playing around back there!" His aunt fingered the rosary hanging around Ennie's neck. "We need to take you to church, to teach you some respect."

"It was my fault," Kelly volunteered suddenly. She had been lingering with fingers clasped through the chain-link fence at the end of the walkway.

Ennie looked over at her, stunned. It was a bold-faced lie and she knew it.

Lucía dropped his arm and stood up for a moment, surveying the grubby girl she hadn't noticed before.

"Who's your girlfriend, Ennie?"

Ennie blushed. He'd never had a girlfriend.

Kelly stuck out a grimy hand, which Lucía eyed suspiciously. Kelly gave up and dropped it to her side. "I'm Kelly," she announced.

"Well, Kelly," Lucía said. "Time for you to go home. Enrique's got to get cleaned up."

Ennie saw Kelly's eyes fall, and he knew why.

"Kelly doesn't have nowhere to go," he said.

"Is that right?" Lucía said.

"Well, sorta," Kelly rubbed some of the dirt off the backs of her fingers. "I ain't going home tonight."

"Are you hungry, Kelly? You would like some dinner, yes?"

Kelly nodded eagerly.

"My *mole* is spicy for a white girl," she said. "I hope you can handle Mexican cooking."

"I can eat spicy," Kelly claimed. "And I'm starved."

"Well, wash up, then. Those filthy hands aren't going anywhere near my food."

"Thanks, *tía*." Kelly winked at Ennie. She followed the older woman up the steps and into the townhouse.

4

"Team up! One on ones!" Steve-O called out.

Steve-O had a bald head and a goatee that was just starting to speckle gray. The burly, Black counselor was a former college player. Word around camp was that he had even gotten a tryout for the Trail Blazers once. More importantly, he was in charge of picking out which of the campers would be selected for rep league in the fall. It all depended on how they performed in the big final on Friday afternoon.

Ennie glanced nervously across the gym at Troy practicing layups. Coming into the week, he'd been confident that he had a good chance to make rep, but Troy had changed everything. Ennie scanned the rest of the gym for another partner, someone he would look good against.

His eyes fell on a chubby, blond kid named Shane. Shane didn't look like he was very good. Ennie started walking across the gym towards him. But a ball bounced loose, and when Ennie ran over to save it, he found Steve-O looming over him.

"Ennie, I want you back with Troy, okay? His size is a good matchup for your speed."

Ennie groaned. "But I was going to—"

"Hey, listen to me." Steve-O wasn't that tall for a baller, but he had a way of dominating every room he stepped into. Right now, Ennie was squarely in his sights. "If you want to be serious about playing ball, you've got to beat the best guy on the floor, right?"

Ennie nodded and dragged his feet towards the far basket. After the Gatorade incident yesterday, Steve-O had made Troy run laps. Troy's hate for Ennie had only doubled since then. His pale arms and legs seemed to stretch out and consume everything around them like a boa constrictor.

"Here," he said, throwing the ball at Ennie's chest. "I'll let you start with the ball today. But I'm still gonna shut you out again."

Ennie had always been pretty good with his bounce. He worked the ball between his legs as he probed from one side of the court to the other for an opening. But Troy kept up with him every step of the way. When he finally turned to drive towards the rim, the ball slipped off his fingertips and hit his toe, rolling harmlessly out of bounds. As Ennie chased after the ball, he heard Troy laughing behind him. He felt like everyone in the gym was watching him fail.

"He's tough," a voice rang out from across the room. Steve-O stood against the white brick wall of the gym, observing. "Let's focus on your dribble. Less fancy back-and-forth, more effort towards the basket."

"That's what I'm *trying* to do," Ennie protested.

"Here, let me check in for a second."

Ennie shrugged and tossed the ball to him. Steve-O crouched low to the ground, dribbling right-handed and using his left arm to protect the ball. He pushed right through Troy to score an easy layup. Troy didn't even have a chance to swipe at the ball before he fell flat on his backside. He picked himself up off the floor and glared at Ennie.

"You're amazing," Ennie said, slack-jawed. He'd never seen a pro move like that before.

"It's nothing," Steve-O handed the ball back to Ennie. "Just get the idea. Troy's got height on you, but if you protect the ball he can't do anything about your speed."

Ennie reset at the top of the key. Troy loomed over him, scowling. Ennie tried to ignore him and focus on technique. He held his left arm over his dribble as he drove towards the basket. He got free for a split second, but then Troy recovered and slapped down hard on his arm. The ball dribbled to the baseline.

"Ow!" Ennie said, shaking out his arm. The cut on his elbow had started bleeding again from the force of the blow.

"Foul!" Steve-O called from the far side of the gym, where he had already turned his attention to helping

Shane with his dribble. His eyes twinkled as he flashed Ennie a pearly white smile.

"Well, you've got him fouling," Steve-O said. "That's step one, at least."

5

Ennie sulked in the car all the way home from camp. It had all gone downhill after that first foul. Troy was still bigger than he was and Ennie had lost the scrimmage by seven points. He could feel Lucía's eyes on him as he stared out the window.

"Something eating at you, *chamaco?*"

"It's nothing."

Ennie didn't want to admit to his *tía* that he wasn't the best kid in camp. For as long as he could remember,

Lucía had listened to him brag about how he was going to be the next Westbrook. And now here he was — a nobody.

His aunt tut-tutted and they drove the rest of the way in silence. When they got back to the townhouse, Ennie bolted straight for the basketball they always kept under the back porch. But Lucía closed the fence and blocked his path.

"Nuh-uh! You've been playing ball all day. Right now, you're going help your *tía* with her *pico*."

His aunt was famous around the block for her *pico de gallo*. Ennie had been learning how to make the traditional Mexican salsa since kindergarten. He groaned, but there was nothing he could do. He followed his aunt into the kitchen and started slicing tomatoes and onions. It seemed like it would definitely get dark before he was done, but eventually he was finished with his cutting. His aunt mixed all the ingredients together in a ceramic bowl.

"Okay, go ahead," she said. "But dinner will be ready in an hour, you hear? Don't stray too far."

Ennie rolled his eyes and said of course he wouldn't. As he dribbled the ball up the sidewalk, he concocted all sorts of crazy scenarios in his head where he could beat Troy. He fantasized about shooting fadeaways, about dribbling through Troy's legs, about alley-ooping to himself off the backboard. He had almost reached the courts by the elementary school when he felt something on his back. He realized he didn't have his ball anymore.

"Hey!" Ennie yelled.

He took off at a dead run after the thief. It was only when he tackled the offender that he realized it was Kelly.

"Hey, superstar." She climbed to her feet, still holding the ball out of his reach. "Gonna go practice your moves?"

"Yeah," Ennie said. "Now give me my ball back."

"You any good for real?" she said. She bounced the ball awkwardly and Ennie swiped it back.

"Better than you," he said. "I play like Westbrook."

"Yeah, right," she said, following him over to the courts.

All the way across the playground Ennie had to protect the ball from Kelly's prying hands, but when they got to the baskets she suddenly sat cross-legged on the concrete.

"I ain't never learned how to play," she admitted.

With her sitting there quietly, Ennie practiced by himself. He imagined cutting through the air like Westbrook for thunderous dunk after thunderous dunk. Mostly, he fantasized about Troy's enormous body falling away from him uselessly.

It was easy to score on an open bucket, and soon Ennie had almost forgotten that Kelly was still there. He scored six straight times before he was startled out of his zone by a loud yawn.

"You ain't so bad, I guess," Kelly said. "But I'm bored. You wanna do something else?"

"Like what?"

"I got a crazy idea. Come on."

6

Ennie was already starting to get the feeling that Kelly was always up to something. But up to something or not, she seemed more interesting than any of the girls he was used to seeing at school, girls who were only interested in talking about their favorite TV show or giggling about makeup.

He followed Kelly down side roads. With each step, they seemed to be getting further from Lucía's. Soon, they passed the Chinese restaurant that marked the end of the block. Ennie was just about to tell her that they should turn around and go back when Kelly turned down a dingy alley.

In this particular alley, the doors on most of the garages had been left open and a collection of carpentry tools seemed to be scattered aimlessly on the concrete. Ennie bounced his ball off the back of a half-constructed dresser. Kelly turned and held her finger up to her mouth.

"My pops always passes out in the middle of the afternoon," she whispered. "The trick is don't wake him up."

"What are we doing?"

"Let's go."

They came to a garage stained with red graffiti and missing the bottom panel. Kelly grabbed the basketball and rolled it through the gap, then scurried through herself. She motioned for Ennie to follow. Once inside, he saw that they were in a sparse garage with a dusty workbench on one side. The workbench had a rusted metal clamp on top and everything on that half of the garage was covered in tiny woodchips.

The other side of the space was bare except for a motorbike. The bike had luscious black leather saddlebags and an exhaust pipe that gleamed a shade of silver that almost reflected Ennie's face in it. Even at a standstill, the vehicle seemed to radiate power. It was the kind of bike Ennie had seen mysterious figures in leather jackets ride down the highway. He'd never seen one up close.

"Can I touch it?" Ennie asked.

"Touch it? We ain't gonna touch it, we're gonna ride it," Kelly whispered. "The keys is inside by the fridge."

Ennie swallowed. "Keys?"

"Yeah, you know what keys look like, don't ya? Fridge is here," she motioned with her hand. "Keys are over here, on the left. Can you remember that?"

"Think so," Ennie said.

"Awright. I'll stand guard out here."

Ennie nodded obediently. He kicked off his Jordans and gently pulled on the screen door leading into the house. It squealed in protest and Ennie froze. He looked back at Kelly nervously. When no sounds came from inside, he tiptoed forward and came to an inside door. It opened into a single, carpeted room.

He felt his heart swallow itself. He could see the fridge on the far side of the apartment, but first he would have to get past a flat-screen TV blaring football highlights and an enormous man with a walrus moustache sprawled on a Lazy Boy. The man's moustache was pointed towards the ceiling. From the mouth hiding inside it, Ennie could hear the rattle of the big man's snores. This must be Kelly's pops.

Ennie's almost turned around and went back, but something stopped him. Going back would be giving up. Kelly would think worse of him if he went back without getting the keys. Ennie didn't want to think of himself as a quitter. He got down on his hands and knees and crawled past the snoring man. He moved silent and quick like an assassin, and in no time at all he'd made it to the fridge.

Nervously, with one eye on Kelly's father, he reached up to grab the keys off the counter. But his reach was off by just a few inches and the ring of keys clattered to the floor. The walrus man groaned, opening one eye and rolling over in his chair.

Ennie squatted on his toes, preparing for a mad dash out of the apartment, but the man settled back into position. It wasn't long before he was happily snoring again. Ennie picked up the keys and darted back to the garage.

"I think I woke him up," he gasped.

7

Kelly hammered the garage door opener with her fist and the machinery came to life. As the door panel loudly opened, Ennie was sure that the racket would wake her pops. Kelly climbed on top of the bike and started fumbling with the ring of keys.

"Do you know what you're doing?" Ennie asked.

"No!" she shrieked. "Makes it fun that way!"

"I dunno about this," Ennie said.

"Get on!" Kelly yelled. Finally she found the right key and jammed it into the ignition. The bike roared to life, but didn't move. She banged on the metal handlebars. "Why ain't it going anywhere?"

"Don't you know how to drive?"

"Sure," Kelly yelled. But it was obvious she was having trouble with the machine.

Over the many sounds filling the garage, Ennie heard the screen door slam behind him. He turned to discover the walrus man blocking the doorframe. His eyes were angry little slits and his round face was blotched red.

"Kelly!" the man yelled. "Get off my bike!"

Ennie bolted through the open garage door. He was sure the enormous man would track him down at any moment, but there was no sign of Kelly or her father.

He ran blindly until he stumbled across the Chinese restaurant. He waited around in front of it for a few minutes, catching his breath and hoping Kelly would show up on her motorbike, but she was nowhere to be found. Soon, he gave up and started the long walk back home.

8

Lucía was waiting for him on the stoop.

"I said one hour, Enrique!"

"Sorry, *tía*."

The large woman sized up Ennie's sorry state. She brushed some sawdust off his t-shirt. "What happened to your ball?"

Ennie suddenly remembered the basketball he'd been bouncing all the way to Kelly's place. It was still somewhere in the garage.

"I don't know," Ennie admitted.

"Enrique. Have you been playing around with that grimy *gringo* again?"

"We were only—" Ennie stopped.

It was strange. While he'd been following Kelly around, it had all seemed like just foolish fun. But now that he was standing in front of Lucía, he knew she wouldn't see it that way.

"I did something dumb, *tía*."

"What is it, child?" she asked softly.

Staring down at the concrete, he confessed to the prank. When he mentioned the bike, his aunt turned his face up towards hers and opened her eyes wide.

"Por favor! That little girl was going to drive a motorcycle?" When Ennie nodded, Lucía took hold of his short, thin hair by the crown. *"Chamaco baboso!* That girl, she's no good for you. She's not from a good Christian

family like us. Don't you forget where you come from, Enrique."

Ennie blushed and looked down at his sneakers. "Yes, *tía.*"

9

Steve-O held the basketball in the palm of his hand and gestured for Ennie to take a seat on the floor of the gym. Ennie could feel the sweat pooling in the collar of his shirt.

The campers had just played two-on-twos. Ennie and Shane had been matched up with Troy and a wiry, rat-tailed kid named Martin. Martin wasn't as good as Troy, but he had a mean streak. Every time Ennie touched the ball, Martin clawed at his shirt or tried to stamp on his feet.

At one point, Ennie fell flat on his face. He felt Martin's hot breath in his ear. "Better luck next time," he snarled.

Martin might play dirty, but Ennie could still outrun him. He started weaving around Martin, scoring a couple of buckets on the rat-tailed teenager. But then Troy switched over to guard him and he didn't stand a chance. Troy swatted one of his shots away. He picked up the bounding ball at the top of the circle and casually nailed a jumper.

After that, Ennie tried to find Shane with the ball, but Shane couldn't score on anything that wasn't right under the hoop. Troy made layup after layup, and when Ennie leaped to try to block a shot, he just laughed.

"You can't touch me," he taunted.

Once the game was over, Steve-O let the other three kids go outside for lunch. But when Ennie tried to follow, the thick-set coach called him back. Ennie took a seat on the floor near the white free throw stripe.

"Do you know why I wanted to talk to you?" Steve-O asked him.

"No," Ennie admitted. "Because I lost?"

Steve-O laughed and shook his head. "Not quite. I hear you've been getting up to some things. Stealing motorcycles? You think you're old enough for that nonsense?"

Ennie shrugged. "It was just some messing around."

"I'm sure it was." Steve-O looked down at Ennie with a sly smile. "I was watching you out there, Ennie. I know Troy's tough. But two-on-two was supposed to level the field."

"What do you mean?"

"What position do you play?"

"Westbrook plays point," Ennie said. "I guess I play point too."

"Exactly. You're a point guard. And do you know what the point guard's number one job is?"

Ennie looked around. More than anything, he wanted to be on the lawn out front of the community center, eating lunch with all the other kids. He threw his hands up in the air. "To pass the ball?"

"Not just pass." Steve-O crouched down and jabbed a finger toward Ennie's left eye. Ennie blinked. "A point's number one job is to see."

"To see? I can see okay."

"I'm talking about seeing the floor. Understanding what's going to happen next. You've got to *have vision*."

"But I'm fast," Ennie said. "You said that was my skill."

"Speed is good, but vision is better. And after vision, you know what a point guard's number two job is?"

Ennie sighed, accepting his fate. "I dunno. Hearing?"

"No." Steve-O handed him the basketball. "Tell me whose ball that is."

"Mine?"

"And you are?"

"The point guard."

"Exactly. Your second job is to *take control*. That means that you're in charge of the ball. Your job is to always be making the right decision."

"Got it," Ennie said, standing up with an eye towards the door. "Have vision. Take control. Can I go eat now?"

"It's not just basketball," Steve-O said. "You take those two things out into the world and you're going to do better in life. Think about that silly prank you played the other night. Did you have vision? Did you have control of the situation?"

Ennie sighed. It was hard to argue with Steve-O, partly because he was so intimidating, but also because Ennie was starting to get the feeling that Steve-O was looking out for him. He had to admit that in hindsight, the whole business with the motorcycle seemed a little ridiculous.

"Probably not," Ennie admitted.

"Now, tomorrow's Friday," Steve-O said. "You can show up for the final and keep playing like you've been playing all week, and you'll probably lose, because Troy's tough. But if you show up ready to play your best game, then you could be unstoppable. And you know what? You just might win."

Ennie blushed. "You think so?"

"Only one way to find out, kiddo."

Ennie escaped the gym gratefully. As he took a seat on the lawn with the other kids, he could still hear Steve-O's words in his head. *Have vision*, he thought. *Take control.* It didn't sound so hard. He took a bite of the burrito his aunt had packed in his lunch bag and tried to figure out how in the world he could put Steve-O's advice into action.

10

After Lucía went to bed that night, Ennie snuck out the back door. In the dark, it was hard to find a solid footing in the cluttered alleyway. Ennie stumbled over pieces of metal and brick as he picked his way towards the old car wreck. He found Kelly curled up under the filthy blanket in the backseat. He banged on the metal husk to wake her up. The next thing he knew, the barrel of the BB gun was pressed against his cheek.

"Aw, sorry, Ennie," she said. "You scared me."

"I snuck out after my aunt went to bed," Ennie said glumly. "But she says I'm not supposed to see you no more."

"You plannin' to listen?"

"I dunno. Everyone's telling me we shouldn't have tried to take that bike."

"I know. I was just bein' dumb," she said, tossing the BB gun into the weeds under the back seat. Ennie started to crawl in next to her but she grabbed hold of him and started to cry into his ratty t-shirt. "I'm scared," she sobbed. "I can't go back there. I'm gonna be stuck in this stupid car for the rest of my life."

Ennie was shocked. Until now, Kelly had seemed too tough to cry. Now it felt like she was holding onto him for dear life. He had no idea how to comfort her. He glanced down in the direction where she'd thrown the gun and recognized a familiar Spalding logo, a little more scuffed up than he remembered it.

"Is that my...?"

"I was gonna bring your ball back for you, superstar." Kelly wiped her eyes. "But I never got around to it. You wanna show me how to play?"

"Right now?"

"Ain't no better time. My pops will probably kill me by tomorrow."

Ennie realized that he needed to do something to cheer Kelly up. Her whole personality seemed like it had changed — she didn't have the spark in her eye anymore. As they made their way through the junk in the alley and back out to the road, Ennie caught a look at her under the streetlight. She always looked grubby, but she looked even worse now. Her face was all scratched up and one of her eyes was swollen. She caught Ennie staring at her and started walking faster.

There weren't any lights at the court outside the school. In the darkness, Kelly awkwardly palmed the ball, then heaved it hopelessly towards the distant outline of the rim. It missed, rattling into the chain-link fence. Ennie chased it down.

"You shoot like this," he whispered gently. He spun the ball off his fingertips. "Let it roll a bit."

She imitated his shot into the empty space in front of her. Then she followed Ennie under the basket and spun the ball off the backboard and through the cylinder.

Her sad face cracked into a gawky, open-mouthed smile that looked a little more like the Kelly from before.

"See, it's fun, right?" he said.

"Yeah, guess so," Kelly said.

11

After that first shot, they played back and forth in the dark in a friendly game of one-on-one. Ennie let Kelly score every time she got the ball. When he had it he tried to make impossible circus shots in the dark to show off. It didn't bother him that she was scoring more than him, but then she got a wacky grin on her face and started bragging.

"Maybe you ain't so hot after all, Ennie!" she squealed after making another bucket. "I got your number."

"As *if*," he said. He decided to score on this possession just to show her he was taking it easy. "Get ready for the Westbrook!" he shouted.

He reset the ball at the top of the key and lined himself up for an easy layup. He drove into the lane but in the darkness, he ran right into Kelly. They collapsed on top of one another in a heap of tangled arms and legs. Ennie felt the soft heat of her cheek against his and realized that his whole body felt as if it was burning up.

"See," she said. "You can't do nothing on me."

"I tripped," Ennie protested. But with her pockmarked little face smiling up at him and their bodies so close together, he wasn't thinking about basketball. He leaned in suddenly and gave Kelly a peck on the lips.

"Ew!" She spat him out. Then she giggled, and it was the girliest sound Ennie had ever heard come out of her mouth. "You're a weird dude, Enrique."

"Sorry." Ennie felt like he'd been sent to the principal's office. His aunt was the only person who called him by his full name. "I didn't mean... We were just so close... I guess I like you."

"You're awright, Ennie," Kelly said. "But whatcha trying to pull?"

"I dunno," Ennie said.

"Anyway, I thought we ain't supposed to hang out."

"I guess I wanna hang out with you," Ennie said. "Even if we gotta sneak around behind my aunt."

"Well, guess I hope we do," she said after a moment. "I get pretty lonely in that car."

"You know, if I gotta be sneaking out anyway..." A thought had occurred to Ennie and he couldn't shake it. "I guess I could probably sneak you in, too. I got a big closet and my aunt never comes to my room."

"For real? That gonna work?"

Ennie had no idea if it would. But it was clear that Kelly couldn't keep sleeping in a car with no one to take care of her. She might seem wild and street-smart, but she wasn't old enough to get by on her own.

"We'll make it work," Ennie said, with a confidence he did not feel.

"Awright," she said. "I don't want to stay in that car no more."

Neither of them was interested in playing basketball anymore. Kelly took Ennie's hand and held it tight as they walked back towards the townhouse. Ennie shushed her and crept up the back porch to make sure the way was clear. He came back to tell her to come on in. But they had only made it to the white plastic kitchen table when the staircase light switched on.

"Darn," Ennie said.

"Enrique." Lucía's thick body loomed on the staircase, her eyes droopy and her dreads wrapped in a checkered green bandana. "What time is it?"

"Sorry, *tía*..."

Then Lucía spotted Kelly lurking behind him.

"*¡Oye!* What did I tell you about running around with *la güera?*"

Ennie swallowed. "She needs our help, *tía*."

"Oh, is that right? A bath is what she needs."

"I can go, miss." Kelly stepped back towards the doorway.

"What kind of help is it you need?" Lucía looked at Kelly severely. "Have you been getting up to any more funny business? Stealing cars now, is it?"

"No. It's my pops," Kelly said. She walked closer so Lucía could hear her better. "My pops told me he ain't never wanna see me again. I think he means it this time."

"*¡Ayyy!* What happened to you?" Lucía's rough fingers explored the marks on Kelly's face. Her words were sharp, but her touch was tender.

Kelly stared at the railing. "He real mad."

"That's not right," Lucía said. "You deserve love, my darling." She turned and frowned at Ennie. *"You* get yourself changed for bed, *niño*. We'll talk about you sneaking around behind my back later."

As Ennie sullenly trudged up the steps towards his bedroom, he heard the water running in the tub and the warm, comforting sound of his aunt cooing over Kelly's injuries.

12

When Ennie woke up in the morning, Kelly was gone. Once he'd satisfied himself that his aunt hadn't hidden her somewhere in the townhouse, he galloped down the alley to check behind the warehouse. But the old Toyota was just a pile of ratty blankets like they'd left it the night before. Ennie stormed into the kitchen.

"Where is she?" he shouted.

Lucía set a chorizo plate on the plastic table in front of him and settled heftily into a chair. She didn't seem bothered by the fact that Ennie was screaming at her.

"None of your business, Enrique. I told you that you weren't going to waste your time with that *gringo* and I mean it."

"But *tía*—"

"You've got the big game this afternoon, remember? You better get that little girl out of your mind and focus on what's important in your life, *sí?*"

"You can't take her away," Ennie said. "She *needs* me."

"*You* need to start thinking about yourself, Enrique. You're too young to go around trying to save other people."

"But she can't go back to her pops!" Ennie shouted. "Can't you see that?"

Lucía sighed. "Eat up. I'm coming this afternoon and I don't want to see my Enrique tired out because he didn't eat his breakfast."

"If I play bad, it'll be your fault."

But Lucía wasn't wrong. Today was Friday, and it was his last chance to show Steve-O what he was made of. Kelly was important, but Kelly would have to wait until after the game today.

Ennie shot his aunt a glare. "It's not fair," he said.

"Life, it is not fair." Lucía stood up from the table and gathered her purse. "I can't expect you to understand. I cannot afford to take a child, not one as wild as that girl."

Ennie stared quietly into his plate of food. He just couldn't get a bad taste out of his mouth. He could barely get any of his breakfast down.

"The worst part is that she didn't even say goodbye," he finally said.

13

The last day of camp was a big production. The gym at the community center had been rigged with temporary bleachers and friends and family would be bringing in folding chairs and banners to tape to the walls after lunch. Steve-O set up a scorer's table. A big, numbered folding scorecard sat mid-court, and a big cardboard box behind him hinted at the trophies that would be handed out to the winning team.

A buzz echoed up to the rafters of the gym. Ennie heard little kids who hadn't made a single basket all week bragging that today was their chance to shine. He wondered if he was just another player who thought he was better than he really was.

The campers spent the morning working out in pairs and watching NBA highlights on YouTube. Ennie worked with Gabby, the only girl in camp. Gabby was a brown-haired eleven-year-old who still had a bit of baby fat on her cheeks. Even though she didn't move very fast, her shot was better than Ennie expected.

Towards lunch, Steve-O gathered everyone around and tried to give a lecture on sportsmanship, but it was no use. It was the last day of camp and everyone was already making plans for the rest of the summer. Two minutes into Steve-O's talk, Troy and Martin started wrestling in the back of the crowd. Steve-O gave up on his speech.

The campers went for lunch after that. When Steve-O called them back inside for their final warm-ups before the big game, he stopped Ennie in the doorway of the gym.

"You ready to win?" he asked.

Ennie shrugged. "I think so."

"Well, *know* so." Steve-O pulled Ennie behind the thick metal doorframe to let the rest of the campers trickle by. "The thing you've got to understand about Troy is that he'll never be better than he is right now. He's peaked. You haven't yet."

"Thanks," Ennie said. He turned away from the coach, but he could feel his cheeks color at the compliment.

The first handful of spectators had already started entering the gym. Ennie heard a whoop, and when he looked over he saw two blonde girls who looked like high schoolers. They were whispering to each other and pointing at Troy. As more people filtered in, Ennie began to see that Troy had his own little fan club.

Eventually, Lucía appeared and climbed to a seat in the back row. She winked at Ennie, but he wanted no part of it. He wished Kelly was there instead of his aunt. As he thought about Kelly, his cheeks burned. The thought of her touch made his skin tingle in ways he didn't understand.

"Welcome, everyone," Steve-O boomed. His powerful voice stopped the rustling and whispering in the crowd immediately. "Let's play some hoops!"

14

The game was three on three. The first team to score eleven baskets won.

Ennie lined up beside Gabby and Shane. The younger campers sat on the bench expectantly. Across the court, Troy and Martin had been teamed with a burly kid named Devon. Devon was good at knocking people over, but not much else. Seeing the two teams lined up, Ennie's heart sank. Troy was looming, but worse, his whole team was going to play dirty.

After Troy won the tip-off, Martin picked up the ball. He flashed his toothy, raccoon grin at Ennie and tried to dribble behind his back to show off for the girls, but he lost control. Ennie dove headlong towards the ball and came face-to-face with Devon's enormous backside. He heard a roar from the bleachers and turned to see Troy score a point.

Ennie picked himself up and thought about Steve-O's words of advice. *Have vision.* How was he supposed to have better vision than that? He'd seen the ball come loose, but he hadn't been quick enough to take advantage.

On the following play, Ennie took the ball at the top of the circle and tried to pull off the stiff-arm move that Steve-O had shown him. But Troy was ready for it. He swatted the ball loose and ran up the court for another basket.

Soon the ball came back to Ennie. As he tried to pass it to Gabby, a hard shove from behind sent him sprawling. Martin passed the ball to Troy under the hoop again.

"That was a foul!" Ennie complained, but Devon's wide frame had blocked Martin's dirty play from Steve-O's vision. No foul was called.

"You're loooo-sing," Martin taunted. He flexed a wiry bicep.

Ennie looked around at his teammates, but they stared back blankly. Devon and Gabby were counting on him. He looked up at the crowd. His aunt waved, but he wasn't really looking for her.

He wondered where Kelly was right this minute. Suddenly, he realized Kelly was what this game was missing. Kelly didn't mind getting in a little trouble. If these guys were going to play dirty, then Kelly would know how to meet them on their own turf.

The time was now. Martin came up the floor with the ball, but Ennie watched Troy, anticipating his next move. When the older kid came hurtling down the lane, Ennie made sure his left leg wandered into Troy's path. Troy stumbled. Ennie picked the ball up and blazed down the court to score a point.

"That's the only one you'll get," Troy growled.

Now it was 3-1. If nothing else, Ennie had shown that he wouldn't back down. And that first point was everything. Ennie knew that if he got completely shut out in front of this many people, he might as well crawl into a hole and forget about basketball forever.

Troy scored again, but as Ennie watched the play unfold, he understood exactly where his teammate's defense had broken down. Ennie might be losing, but at least he was seeing the floor.

15

Take control. Ennie remembered Steve-O's second piece of advice.

As he dribbled, Ennie forgot that there was even a crowd in the gym. He wasn't aware of anything except the ball and the five other players. When Troy and Devon tried to take the ball, he sensed that Gabby was open. He threw her the ball and she made the shot.

"Just lucky," Martin sneered.

"This is where I start trying," Troy said menacingly. "Don't start thinking I'm going to let you win."

On the next play, Troy pushed through Ennie and scored. But something had changed. Ennie wasn't scared of Troy. He started focusing for his teammates instead. They weren't the most talented players, but they could make shots when they were open. He made a pass to Shane this time, who dunked the ball.

The game went back and forth for a while. Ennie wasn't paying attention to the score, but he knew it was close. Troy had finally stopped wasting his breath on trash talk. The effort of scoring all those points was starting to wear him down.

Ennie made a beeline for the basket. His dribble seemed to linger in the air as it traveled up and down his lanky frame. Troy got in front of Ennie, and for an instant, time seemed to slow to a crawl. It was as if Troy was moving in slow motion. Ennie crossed left and Troy lost his footing trying to block Ennie. His tall, skinny body crashed to the floor like a bowling pin. Ennie glided past him for an easy score.

"Time out!" Troy yelled. "Time out! He hurt me!"

For the first time in several minutes, Ennie became aware of the crowd. He heard a whole lot of raucous screaming and cheering — and at least a couple of people booing.

"That's it!" Steve-O boomed. "That's eleven!"

"I said time out!" Troy screamed. "That was a foul!"

He lay on the floor, holding his left thigh. Ennie noticed that his face had turned red and tears had started to stream down his cheeks. Lying there like that, he suddenly didn't seem so invincible.

"You figured it out!" Steve-O was shaking his shoulders. "You got it!"

Troy picked himself off the floor and stormed out of the gym before the trophies could be awarded. No one followed him. Not even Martin or the blonde girls who'd been giggling about him before the game. Now that he'd finally lost, it seemed like no one liked him anymore.

Ennie walked over to the bench in a daze. The younger kids mobbed around him, congratulating him on the victory. Shane wiped some sweat from his brow with a chubby, freckled arm and gave Ennie a high-five. Gabby walked up and shyly gave him a hug.

Then it was time for the trophy ceremony. Ennie accepted his gold figurine from Steve-O, but he still couldn't process what had happened on the last play. He knew that he'd won, but how had he contorted Troy's body in slow motion like that?

As he wondered, he felt Lucía's embrace swallow him up.

"You did it, *esquincle*," she shrieked. "You won!"

"Yeah, I won," Ennie repeated, but in the moment after the thrill of his victory faded, he remembered that Kelly was gone. He frowned at his aunt. "No thanks to you."

"What's wrong, child?" she said. "Aren't you happy?"

"You shouldn't have sent her away like that." Ennie said. "She should be here for this."

"Oh, shush," Lucía muttered quietly. "Just enjoy your victory, Enrique."

16

Ennie stayed mad about Kelly for a while, but the summer moved on without her. After camp ended, Steve-O started coming by the court at the school to help Ennie with his shot.

Ennie had locked up his spot on the team, but he still didn't stand a chance when it came to stopping Steve-O. The old coach liked to show off with fadeaway jumps and slick crossovers that left Ennie in his dust. Ennie had to admit their scrimmages were good practice for the competition he would be facing in the fall.

Near the end of the summer, the city cleared out the alleyway behind the warehouse. Ennie watched a parade of burly men march past his door, filling enormous metal garbage bins with all the junk. The old Toyota was the first thing to go, towed away before the men even showed up. Soon, all traces of the old junk pile were gone. They even ripped up the broken-down wire fence.

On the last Sunday before the Labor Day weekend, as Lucía was getting Ennie dressed for church, Steve-O came by the townhouse and told Ennie he had some bad news.

"It looks like I'm not going to be coaching you after all," he said, his calm, brown eyes twinkling above his salt-and-pepper goatee. "I got offered an assistant coaching job at Springfield College."

"That's great!" Lucía said. "Isn't that great, Ennie?"

Ennie wasn't so sure. Steve-O had been his only constant all summer. His coaching had made Ennie a better player. And whatever it was that he had done to Troy that Friday afternoon at the gym didn't seem like the sort of thing he could count on. He was looking forward to having a coach around who could bring that out of him again.

"It's a small school," Steve-O said demurely. "Still, it's an opportunity."

"Well, we're just getting ready for church," Lucía said. "But do you want to come in for a Coke?"

"I have to pack up today," Steve-O said. "New England's a long flight."

"How come you took my side?" Ennie blurted out. He didn't know how to tell Steve-O not to leave him behind.

"It's simple," Steve-O said. "I saw something in you. Guys like Troy — they're a dime a dozen. I remember guys like him from back when I was in college. They got some talent, but they think that gives them a right to something."

"Troy, he was a punk," Lucía said, holding Ennie's shoulders from behind. "Anyone could see that."

"I was more like you, Ennie," Steve-O said. "I was undersized and I had to fight to get noticed. And I saw that you were willing to work on improving yourself. That's as important as all the talent in the world."

"Ennie's a good kid," Lucía said. "He might not know it yet, but he is."

His aunt walked the big man out to his truck to thank him for all the extra attention he'd paid Ennie, but Ennie was mad that Steve-O was abandoning him. He slipped out the back way. He was still wearing his crisply ironed church shirt, but he didn't care.

He walked towards the old warehouse. For the first time in his life, he stopped to read the faded yellow sign painted high above him on the white brick. *Tommy's Hardware*, it had once said, but now half the letters were rubbed out and the rest was only an outline.

The alleyway was sparse and empty. The maintenance men had done a thorough job. All that was left of the old clutter was a small pile of smashed bricks that would have been a hassle to pick up. Without all the stuff, the space seemed smaller than he remembered. Then Ennie wondered if maybe he was just bigger than he'd been at the beginning of the summer.

He sat down on a patch of the brown grass poking through the cracks in the cement and sighed. There was no imagining left to be done in this alleyway. It was what it was, just a neglected patch of dirt, grass, and concrete. Ennie kicked at one of the bricks and it split in two and rolled away. A glint of metal shone in the mid-morning sunlight. Ennie dug around it and discovered that for all the junk they'd picked through, the men had missed something.

He picked his old Swiss Army knife out of the dirt. It was crusted with grass and mud, but there wasn't a single spot of rust on the stainless steel and each of the tools still flicked into place cleanly. Ennie jammed the multi-tool into his front shirt pocket and headed back to the townhouse. He hoped that Lucía wouldn't yell at him for being late for church.

Running the Point

17

Ennie took his dribble behind his back, faked a drive at the rim, and pulled back for a fadeaway jumper. The ball rolled all the way around the rim and trickled through the hoop.

"You're too good, man," the dark-skinned kid with a puffy Afro named Juwan said.

After taking over from Steve-O, Mr. Wishek — or Wishbone, as the kids called him — had run the team with an iron fist. Any player who was fifteen minutes late for practice was benched for at least a game, and everyone ran pylon drills at every single practice. The grind was exhausting, but over the last year Ennie had seen his game improve by leaps and bounds.

Troy had been assigned to the same team, but he'd struggled to keep up with the drills. After being benched during a game a month into the season, he'd stormed out of the gym and never returned. For his part, Ennie had earned himself starting point guard duties, but Wishbone told him the last thing he needed to work on was a better outside shot.

"If you want to make varsity as a high school freshman," Wishbone had warned him, "then you need to take your weak hand off the ball."

Here, against Juwan, Ennie was working on properly flicking the wrist of his shooting hand into each shot.

"I quit." Juwan tossed the ball back to Ennie in disgust and sauntered back toward his friends on the other side of the court.

He had a thicker build than Ennie and an attitude, but his slow moves had been no match for the little Mexican. The pass he threw was sloppy and the ball bounded past Ennie out toward the chain-link fence. Ennie put his head down and chased after it, but a teenage girl with her long blonde hair tied back in a ponytail got there first.

"This yours, superstar?"

Ennie did a double take. He recognized the voice, but the girl in front of him looked nothing like the Kelly he remembered. The dirt and the grime were gone. She was scrubbed clean, with shiny, bright-red lipstick and two stud earrings in each ear. Ennie was sure she hadn't had her ears pierced the year before. Kelly had always seemed a few months older than him, but it was still a shock to see her looking almost like a woman.

"Thanks," he said. "I didn't recognize you."

"I know, I look all weird." Her face was bright red, but Ennie couldn't be sure if she was blushing or if it was just her makeup.

"What are you doing here?" Ennie said. "Where's your pops?"

"My pops?" Kelly laughed. "I ain't seen him since the last time I saw you." She pointed out to the street, where a dark-skinned lady in a flower print skirt was leaning against a blue sedan. "That's Sue. She been taking care of me."

"Oh," Ennie said, looking at the ground. "I thought my aunt sent you back to your pops."

"You ain't know?" Kelly said. "Sue's from the church group. Lucía even comes by the house sometimes to bring me clothes and things. I gotta go back to my real mom when she gets out of jail, though."

Ennie suddenly felt embarrassed. He had never really forgiven his aunt for sending Kelly home, but now he realized he'd underestimated Lucía. She might have her own ways, but she meant well.

"Oh," he said again.

Standing here in front of her, Ennie felt like he had so much to say to Kelly, but none of the thoughts seemed to want to turn themselves into words.

18

"Wait here," Kelly said. "I got something for ya."

She took off toward the car, and for a second as she ran, she looked like the tomboy Ennie remembered. But then her feet got tangled in the folds of her skirt and she had to slow down. She jogged back to him carrying a soft bundle wrapped in tissue paper.

"This is for me?" he asked. "How did you — Why?"

"You ain't that hard to find, silly," she said. "We just looked for a basketball court. Now hurry up and open it."

Ennie tore into the paper and uncovered a patch of blinding white fabric. He pulled at it and a full-size, straight-off-the-rack basketball jersey fell into his hands. He turned it over. Above the enormous blue zero in the middle of the back, the word WESTBROOK was sewn in big block letters.

"I'm sorry for tearing up your old magazine," Kelly said. "I had no idea it could mean anything to anyone."

"Thanks!" Ennie said. "I didn't even think you remembered..."

He pulled the jersey over his head. Kelly walked a semicircle around him, inspecting.

"Well, it almost fits. Sue said I gotta leave a little room because you're still growing." Kelly put her mouth up to Ennie's ear. "She also says to take care of it 'cause it's *expensive*." She giggled and stepped away from Ennie. "Sue's rich, you know."

"I will," Ennie assured her. "I'll keep it in perfect condition."

Kelly took hold of Ennie's hand. "Thanks," she said. "Thanks for trying to help me."

"I thought I messed it all up," Ennie said.

"Y'know, if it weren't for you I'd probably be back at my pops' place right now. You got me outta some big trouble, even if you never knew it." She dropped his hand. "Anyway, I just wanted to say bye for real."

Kelly took a step towards the street.

"Wait," Ennie said. "Where are you going?"

"Sue's taking me to see my mom." Kelly stuck out her tongue. "She says I gotta show her how I dress up nice."

"But…" Ennie started, searching for the words. "We gonna see each other again?"

"Maybe," Kelly shrugged. "You're gonna be in high school soon, right? You still gonna let your aunty tell you who you can sneak around with then, superstar?" She threw him a wink. "I'll be around. Or maybe not."

As Kelly strolled back to the car, Ennie wondered if she was leaving his life for good. Without so much as a glance back, she climbed into the passenger side of the vehicle. The car turned out onto the street and disappeared behind an oak tree on the corner.

After it was gone, Ennie looked down at his new jersey once again, touching it to make sure it was real. Then he dribbled a couple of times and turned towards the hoop. He flicked his right hand gently through the ball and watched as it rose in a perfect arc towards the basket and then swished quietly through the mesh — nothing but nylon.

About The Author

Simon Broder is a freelance writer and editor based in Toronto, ON, Canada. His sports writing appears at RaptorsHQ.com and BlueJaysNation.com, and his fiction has previously appeared in Blank Spaces literary journal. Simon also works as a copywriter and ghostwriter and is currently working on a creative non-fiction book project.

About The Publisher

Story Shares is a nonprofit focused on supporting the millions of teens and adults who struggle with reading by creating a new shelf in the library specifically for them. The ever-growing collection features content that is compelling and culturally relevant for teens and adults, yet still readable at a range of lower reading levels.

Story Shares generates content by engaging deeply with writers, bringing together a community to create this new kind of book. With more intriguing and approachable stories to choose from, the teens and adults who have fallen behind are improving their skills and beginning to discover the joy of reading. For more information, visit storyshares.org.

Easy to Read. Hard to Put Down.